My Pal, VICTOR

Mi amigo, Víctor

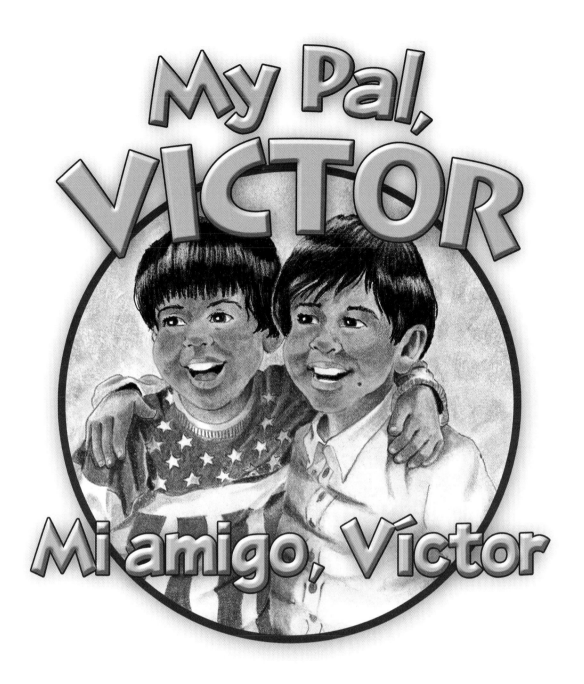

Written by / Escrito por Diane Gonzales Bertrand
Illustrated by / Ilustrado por Robert L. Sweetland
Translated by / Traducción por Eida de la Vega

For my pal, Kathleen M. Muldoon, who inspired this story.
– Diane

To my pal, Nancy.
– Bob

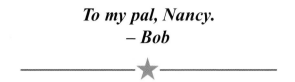

All rights reserved. For information about permission to reproduce selections from this book, write to:
Permissions, Raven Tree Press LLC, 200 S. Washington St. – Suite 306, Green Bay, WI 54301
www.raventreepress.com

Bertrand, Diane Gonzales.

My pal, Victor / written by Diane Gonzales Bertrand ; illustrated
by Robert Sweetland = Mi amigo, Víctor / escrito por Diane
Gonzales Bertrand ; ilustrado por Robert Sweetland ; traducción
al español de Eida de la Vega. — 1st ed. — Green Bay, WI :
Raven Tree Press, 2004, c2003.

    p. cm.

    Audience: grades K-4.
    Text in English and Spanish.
    Summary: Two Latino boys experience carefree camaraderie
despite one boy's disability. Fun and friendship overpower
physical limitations.
    ISBN: 0-9720192-9-4

    1. Friendship—Juvenile fiction. 2. Children with disabilities—
Juvenile fiction. 3. Bilingual books. 4. [Friendship]. I. Sweetland,
Robert. II. Vega, Eida de la. III. Title. IV. Mi amigo, Víctor.

PZ7.B478 2004   2003092133
[E]—dc21   0406

Printed in the U.S.A.
10 9 8 7 6 5 4 3 2 1

first edition

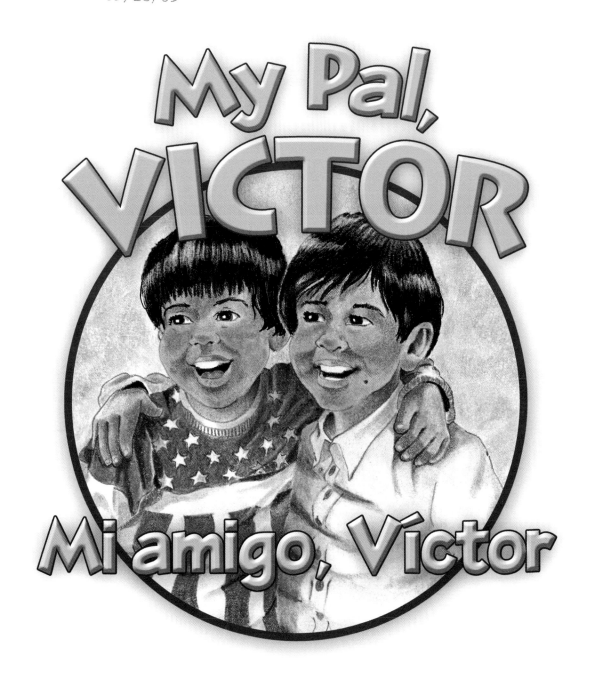

My Pal, VICTOR

Mi amigo, Víctor

Written by / Escrito por **Diane Gonzales Bertrand**
Illustrated by / Ilustrado por **Robert L. Sweetland**
Translated by / Traducción por **Eida de la Vega**

My pal, Victor, makes up great stories.
He points to a cloud and a dragon appears,
or a rocket ship, or the pyramids in Mexico.

———————★———————

Mi amigo Víctor inventa historias fabulosas.
Señala una nube y aparece un dragón,
o un cohete espacial, o las pirámides de México.

5

Sometimes he puts us into his stories.
It's like a movie playing in our heads.

———————★———————

En ocasiones, somos protagonistas de sus historias.
Es como una película que se proyectara en nuestras cabezas.

My pal, Victor, tells great jokes like, "Did you hear about
the chicken who wanted to dance a polka?"
Or, "Why did the elephant paint his toenails red?"

———————★———————

Mi amigo Víctor cuenta muy buenos chistes como: "¿Has oído hablar
del pollo que quería bailar polca?".
O: "¿Por qué el elefante se pinta de rojo las uñas de los pies?".

Or the one that goes: "If you mix a parrot and a pickle together, what do you get?"

———————★———————

O el que dice: "Si cruzas una cotorra y un pepinillo, ¿qué resulta?".

We laugh from joke to joke until our stomachs hurt.

———————★———————

Nos reímos de sus chistes hasta que el estómago comienza a dolernos

My pal, Victor, cheers loudest at my baseball games.
He claps and yells.
He whistles and calls, "Go, Dominic, go!"
as I run around the bases.

———————⭐———————

Mi amigo Víctor es quien más alto vitorea cuando juego al béisbol.
Aplaude y grita.
Silba y me dice, "¡Arriba, Dominic, arriba!",
cuando estoy recorriendo las bases.

And he gives me the high-five when I make it home–SAFE!

————————★————————

Y chocamos las manos cuando llego a home sin que me atrapen.

My pal, Victor, swims better than a fish.
We dive for pennies at the bottom of the pool.
He watches my famous fantastic belly flop.
I clap for his fabulous floating frog stroke.

———————★———————

Mi amigo Victor nada mejor que un pez.
Buceamous hasta el fondo de la piscina en busca de centavos.
Él contempla mi famoso y extraordinario clavado de barriga.
Yo aplaudo su fabulosa brazada de la rana flotadora.

My pal, Victor, whispers scary stories at midnight
when I sleep over at his house.
He puts the flashlight under his chin.

———————★———————

Mi amigo Victor me susurra historias de miedo a medianoche,
cuando me quedo a dormir en su casa.
Se pone la linterna debajo de la barbilla.

He tells heart-booming stories
about ghosts and monsters and haunted houses.
Even my goose bumps get scared!

———————★———————

Cuenta terroríficas historias
de fantasmas y monstruos y casas encantadas.
¡Le mete miedo al susto!

My pal, Victor, loves to ride the highest rollercoasters
and the dizziest, zoomiest, fastest rides he can find.

---★---

A mi amigo Víctor le encanta subir a la montaña rusa más alta
y a los apartos más rápidos, mareantes y vertiginosos
que pueda encontar.

I walk out wobbly and dizzy,
but Victor points out the next ride we need to try.

———————————★———————————

Yo salgo tambaleante y mareado,
pero Víctor señala el próximo aparato que quiere montar.

24

My pal, Victor, throws a toy
for his dog to catch.

———————⭐———————

Mi amigo Víctor le lanza un juguete a su perro
para que éste lo atrape.

He blows big, bubble-gum bubbles.
He feeds the ducks his leftover lunch.

———————★———————

Infla enormes globos con chicle.
Alimenta a los patos con las sobras de su almuerzo.

My pal, Victor, and I do so many fun things.

───────── ★ ─────────

Mi amigo Víctor y yo hacemos muchas cosas divertidas.

29

But, the most important thing about my pal, Victor,
is that he likes me just the way I am.

————————★————————

Pero lo más importante es que yo le gusto tal y como soy.

31

Vocabulary/Vocabulario

English	Español
stories	las historias
cloud	la nube
jokes	los chistes
baseball	el béisbol
fish	el pez
ride	montar
dog	el perro
monsters	los monstruos
important	importante
fun	divertidas

Answers to jokes found in this book are:
page 8   She couldn't find ballet shoes in her size.
page 8   So he could hide in the cherry tree.
page 10 A pickle who wants a cracker.